I think my sister or brother might enjoy reading this story with you!!

Enjoy!
Love, Grama
Julienne
2018

The
Pirate Pig

ALSO BY CORNELIA FUNKE

Emma and the Blue Genie

Ruffleclaw

The Pirate Pig

CORNELIA FUNKE

TRANSLATED BY OLIVER LATSCH

ILLUSTRATED BY KERSTIN MEYER

A YEARLING BOOK

Text copyright © 1999 by Cornelia Funke
Translation copyright © 2015 by Oliver Latsch
Interior illustrations copyright © 1999 by Kerstin Meyer
Cover art copyright © 2015 by Vivienne To

All rights reserved. Published in the United States by Yearling, an imprint of Random House Children's Books, a division of Penguin Random House LLC, New York. Originally published as *Das Piratenschwein* by Cecilie Dressler Verlag GmbH & Co. KG, Hamburg, Germany, in 1999. This translation was originally published in hardcover in the United States by Random House Children's Books, New York, in 2015.

Yearling and the jumping horse design are registered trademarks of Penguin Random House LLC.

Visit us on the Web! randomhousekids.com

Educators and librarians, for a variety of teaching tools, visit us at RHTeachersLibrarians.com

The Library of Congress has cataloged the hardcover edition of this work as follows:
Funke, Cornelia Caroline.
[Piratenschwein. English]
The pirate pig / Cornelia Funke ; translated by Oliver Latsch ; illustrated by Kerstin Meyer.—First American edition.
p. cm.
"Originally published as Das Piratenschwein by Cecilie Dressler Verlag GmbH & Co. KG, Hamburg, Germany, in 1999."—Copyright page.
Summary: On Butterfly Island, sailor Stout Sam and his deckhand, Pip, must rescue their treasure-sniffing pig from nasty pirate Barracuda Bill.
ISBN 978-0-385-37544-3 (trade) — ISBN 978-0-385-37545-0 (pbk.) — ISBN 978-0-385-37546-7 (lib. bdg.) — ISBN 978-0-385-37547-4 (ebook)
[1. Pigs—Fiction. 2. Pirates—Fiction. 3. Buried treasure—Fiction. 4. Islands—Fiction.] I. Latsch, Oliver, translator. II. Meyer, Kerstin, illustrator. III. Title.
PZ7.F96624Pj 2015 [Fic]—dc23 2014000879

MANUFACTURED IN CHINA

10 9 8 7 6 5 4 3 2

First Yearling Edition 2015

This book has been officially leveled by using the F&P Text Level Gradient™ Leveling System.

*For Ben, the little pirate, and for Anna,
who has to look after him sometimes*

manta ray

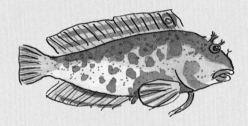

blenny

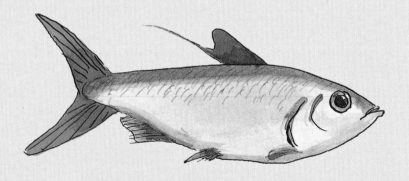

oxeye

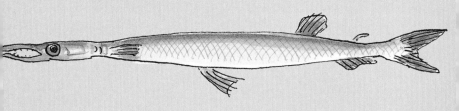

noodlefish

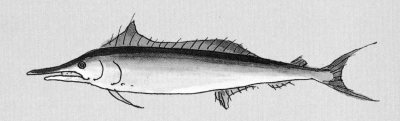

marlin

haddock

On Butterfly Island, everybody knew Stout Sam and his boat with the green sail.

Sam lived together with Pip, his deckhand, on the beach, in a small hut under trees that grew the sweetest fruit on the whole island.

But you can't live on fruit alone.

That's why there was a sign on Sam's hut. It said: ISLAND TRANSPORTS.

Pip had written the sign, while Stout Sam had watched him full of admiration and growled, "Shiver me timbers, boy, those are some devilishly tricky words you're writing there."

The two of them really had a lot to do. Even when it stormed so badly that the jellyfish crawled ashore, Stout Sam and Pip sailed out and took coconuts, or barrels of rum, or crates full of stockfish from one island to the other. Every evening, they returned to their hut, and they felt happy as they climbed into their hammocks.

It was a peaceful life, and they liked it.

But then, one morning, the two decided to take a walk on the beach before work. Stout Sam looked out across the sea, and Pip searched the sand for seashells.

And suddenly the waves washed up a barrel right in front of their feet.

When Pip looked inside the barrel, he found a pig grunting back at him. The pig was barely bigger than a pug, and around its neck hung a gold chain with a skull-and-crossbones pendant.

"Parrot perch and swordfish fins!" said Stout Sam. "We can't leave the wee thing out here, can we, Pip?"

"Out of the question," Pip answered. He lifted the little pig out of the barrel, and they took it back to their hut.

They named the pig Julie. And very soon they realized what they had found was no ordinary pig.

While Julie did enjoy rolling around in the mud as much as other pigs, what she loved most was to sit on the beach and look at the sea. Her favorite food was lugworms with sea grass. And when Pip and Stout Sam sailed between the islands, Julie stood right at the prow of the boat, holding her nose into the salty breeze and grunting with joy.

But Julie wouldn't swim.

Because she was afraid of water. Very afraid.

One day—Julie was still quite a small piglet—Sam and Pip got the job of delivering twenty-three crates of coconuts to the neighboring island.

And that's when it happened: way out on the high sea, Julie suddenly began to squeal. She squealed as though a shark had gotten hold of her curly tail. Then she rushed to the old fishing net that lay bundled up next to the mast and nudged it overboard with her snout.

Sam was dumbfounded. "Thundering typhoons, Julie! What in cod's name has gotten into you?"

But when Pip and Sam pulled the net out of the water, it was full of gleaming gold and silver. Pip had to throw two crates of coconuts into the sea to make space for all the treasure.

"Well, somebody fry me a flounder!" Stout Sam gasped. He tickled Julie behind the ears and said to Pip, "Would you believe it? Our Julie can smell treasure!"

Pip was staring at the chests full of gold and gemstones. He had started to grow a little pale around the nose. "Captain!" he whispered. "I've heard that sometimes pirates catch piglets and train them to smell out treasure. You think Julie could be a . . . p-p-pirate pig?"

Stout Sam spat into the water. "Yes, that's exactly what I think," he growled. "You know what the pirates do to such a pig when it doesn't find them enough treasure?"

Pip shook his head and put his arm around Julie.

"They stick the poor critter into a barrel and throw it overboard. That's what they do, those mean mudsnappers."

Julie pricked her ears and looked at Sam as though she could understand what he was saying.

"Ah! So that's why she has this!" Pip blurted out. He looked at Julie's pendant. "Nasty thugs."

He planted a kiss between Julie's ears and squeezed her very tight. "That won't happen again, Julie," he said. "You can count on that!"

"One hundred percent!" Stout Sam agreed.

And with that they finally sailed on to their destination.

≫ ≫ ≫

Three months passed. Julie grew bigger and rounder, and nearly every week she found another treasure in the sea.

Stout Sam threw most of the things back into the water. Silver goblets, gemstones, earrings . . . what was he going to do with all those trinkets, anyway?

But they kept the gold coins. To buy food for Julie. Because Julie was always hungry.

One day, Stout Sam had an idea. It was a nice idea, but also a stupid idea.

He took three crowns and a couple of yard-long pearl necklaces he and Pip had just fished out of the water and gave them to the kids playing by the docks. Just to make their game of "Pirates and Princesses" a little more fun. That was nice. Very nice.

But still, Sam should not have done that.

Soon enough, word got around that Stout Sam's net caught crowns and pearl necklaces

instead of fish. And then people began to say that it must have had something to do with the pig he always took with him.

"Bah, nonsense!" Stout Sam muttered every time he heard that. "Really, you have to believe me, Julie is just an ordinary pig. Am I right, or am I right, Pip?"

Pip nodded as hard as he could.

But it was useless. Nobody believed them.

In no time, even the fish in the sea knew that Stout Sam had found himself a real pirate pig.

And then the inevitable happened: Barracuda Bill heard about Julie.

Barracuda Bill was the greediest and meanest pirate who had ever sailed the seas between the islands.

"Well, well!" he growled when his coxswain, Swordfish, told him about Julie. "A pirate pig. Didn't One-Eared Ernie throw a pig overboard some time ago?"

"Indeed, Your Nastiness," Swordfish answered, "because it hadn't found any treasure in four months."

"And now that pig finds so much treasure that Stout Sam is throwing jewels by the chestload back into the sea!" whispered Greasebeard, who always carried Barracuda Bill's sword for him.

"Well, it should be obvious what we need to do," said Barracuda Bill. "Am I making myself clear, you deckload of bandy-legged water rats?"

His men grinned so much that all their gold teeth showed. "Clear as crystal, Your Nastiness!" they roared.

And up went the sails.

DYNAM
NO.23

The next evening, Stout Sam decided to go for a walk before bedtime. Pip was already snoring in his hammock, so Julie went along with Sam.

As the two of them strolled along the harbor wall, three of Barracuda Bill's men snuck up from behind. They pushed Sam into the grimy water and dragged the loudly squealing Julie away.

Stout Sam was so upset he tore his favorite shirt to shreds.

He and Pip searched the entire island. They knocked on every door, looked at every pig. Yes, Stout Sam even clambered onto a donkey to search the mountains for Julie.

But they couldn't even find a single one of
Julie's pink bristles.

Brokenhearted, they returned to the harbor.

Their boat looked terribly empty without
Julie.

"Those scoundrels have probably taken her
off the island, Captain!" said Pip as they climbed
aboard. "But we'll carry on searching as soon as
the sun rises again. Maybe she was taken to one
of the volcanic islands in the south. Or to the
mainland."

Stout Sam nodded quietly. He sat down on the deck and stared out at the sea. And even though Pip himself was as sad as he'd ever been in his life, he would have loved to cheer Sam up. But how?

"How 'bout I get us something to eat, Captain?" he suggested.

Stout Sam just shook his head.

"Not hungry," he muttered.

Now Pip was really getting worried.

Over in the Thirsty Shellfish, they served fresh jellyfish cream cake—Stout Sam's favorite. Maybe that would cheer him up.

"I'll be right back, Captain!" Pip called. He reached into the chest with the gold coins and ran off.

⇒ ⇒ ⇒

The Thirsty Shellfish was packed to the eaves, as usual. Pip squeezed through the bellies and elbows until he reached the counter. He ordered twelve jellyfish cream cakes.

The Thirsty Shellfish was run by Lanky Lola.

When she spotted Pip standing by the counter, she went over to hand him the cakes herself.

"Listen!" she whispered to Pip. "You're Stout Sam's shipboy, ain't ya? Tell him Barracuda Bill has your pig. He's got it on his ship. He's been sitting in that corner there all evening, bragging to everybody how the pig is going to make him the biggest pirate of the islands!"

Lanky Lola looked around anxiously and put a finger to her red lips. "You didn't hear it from me, understood, boy?"

And with that, she quickly retreated to the other end of the counter.

Pip scanned the room.

The Red Devil
Barracuda Bill's Pirate Ship

Mast

Yard

Headsail

Figurehead

Bow

Anchor chain

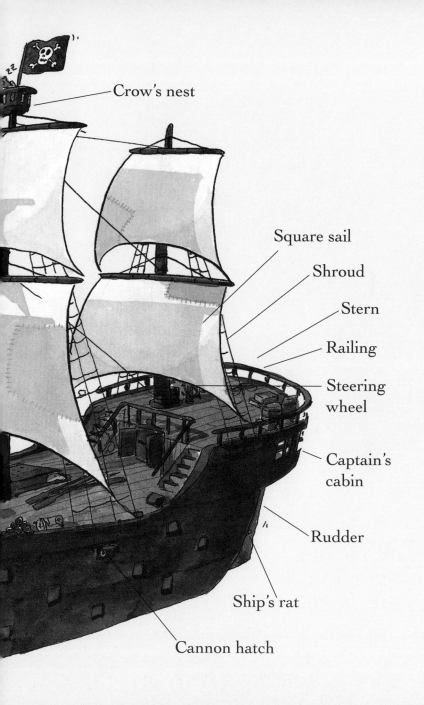

Crow's nest

Square sail

Shroud

Stern

Railing

Steering
wheel

Captain's
cabin

Rudder

Ship's rat

Cannon hatch

He'd never met Barracuda Bill, but everybody knew he was easily recognized by his
golden eye patch.

It was dark and crowded in the
Thirsty Shellfish, and it took Pip a while
to spot him.

Barracuda Bill was sitting with
his men in the darkest corner. They
all looked very wild and danger-
ous. Pip's heart nearly dropped
into the bottom of his pants.

You nasty pig thieves, he
thought. He shot one last
glance in their direction and
then quickly pushed his
way to the exit. His heart
was beating wildly.

All the excitement
made him leave Stout
Sam's jellyfish cream
cakes on the counter.

Pip ran as quickly as his feet would carry him through the dark harbor and past the ships bobbing on the moonlit water. Finally he reached Stout Sam's boat.

"Captain!" Pip panted as he jumped on board. "Captain, I know who stole Julie!"

Stout Sam lifted his head. He'd been shaping pigs from pink marzipan.

"Barracuda Bill took her!" Pip wheezed. "He's sitting in the Thirsty Shellfish, bragging about how he stole her."

Stout Sam had to digest the news for a while. He spat over the railing three times before he regained his voice.

"Thundering tarps!" he said. "The Barracuda. Do you know who we're dealing with here?"

Pip nodded.

With a deep sigh, Stout Sam pushed himself to his feet. "Well, then let's go," he said, putting his arm around Pip's shoulders. "Ready the dinghy. We're taking our pig back."

⇛ ⇛ ⇛

Everybody knew that Barracuda Bill never moored his big ship in the harbor. He preferred to drop anchor out on the open sea and have his men row him to shore in his launch.

"Let's hope the scoundrel didn't leave too many guards on board," Stout Sam whispered as they rowed their boat out of the harbor.

Pip nodded. He peered anxiously into the night. The silence was so scary that his heart began to beat even faster.

Suddenly a ship appeared out of the darkness. Its hull was jet-black, but the deck was well lit by the moon, and the pirate flag fluttered from the highest mast.

"That must be it!" Pip whispered. He barely dared to breathe as Stout Sam steered the dinghy toward the huge ship.

Ropes creaked above them. Two guards were fast asleep in the ship—one on top of the mast and one at the stern. A wooden devil grinned down at Stout Sam and Pip from the bow. From his horns hung a rope ladder.

"Isn't that nice?" Stout Sam whispered. "They left the ladder out. What they can climb down, we can climb up!"

"Did you see?" Pip whispered. "They tied our poor Julie to the railing."

"Miserable pig torturers!" Stout Sam growled. He quickly rowed the boat to the ladder. Its end dangled less than three feet above the water.

"Better I go, Captain," Pip said quietly. "The pirates will be back before you ever manage to heave your big belly up there."

Stout Sam wanted to protest, but Pip was already on the ladder.

"I'll screech like a gull three times if I spot them coming back," Sam quietly called after him.

Pip nodded as he clambered up toward the wooden devil.

The guards were still snoring when Pip swung his legs over the railing. He could clearly see the man up in the crow's nest, but all he could

see of the other man were his naked feet sticking
out from behind a barrel.

Julie lay tied to the railing. Her bristly back
was turned to Pip. He tiptoed toward her and
put his hand over her pink snout.

"Not a peep, Julie!" he whispered. "It's me,
Pip. The captain is also here. We're taking you
home."

Julie made a delighted grunt and nudged her
nose into Pip's belly.

Pip pulled his knife from his belt and began
to saw away at the thick rope. He wasn't making

much headway, because Julie kept nudging and
sniffing him.

"Please stop, Julie!" Pip hissed. "I'll be done
soon."

But just as he managed to cut through the
rope, Pip heard the screech of a gull. Once.
Twice. Three times. Stout Sam was sounding
the alarm!

Pip jumped to the railing and peered into the
night.

He heard oars splashing and loud shouts.

And then he saw a boat appear from the
darkness.

⇒ ⇒ ⇒

Barracuda Bill was standing unsteadily at the bow, holding a lantern. His men barely managed to row in a straight line, but they were coming closer. Quite quickly, actually.

"We have to move, Julie!" Pip hissed. He dragged the pig to the other side of the ship, but as soon as he swung one leg over the railing, Julie jumped back.

"Go, Julie!" Pip called. "Jump! You don't have to be scared. The captain is waiting in the boat."

But the pig stood frozen. And Pip suddenly remembered how much Julie was afraid of water.

"Pip! They're nearly here! Where are you?" he heard Stout Sam call from below.

Pip wanted to answer, but at that moment, the man in the crow's nest woke up. Yawning, he got to his feet and rubbed his puffy eyes. Then he looked out to sea, toward the incoming boat.

39

"Commander returning to ship!" he roared so loudly that Julie's bristles stood on end. "Ready the cannon for the welcome salute!"

As quickly as he could, Pip dragged Julie under a pile of old sails. And not a moment too soon, for when he peered out from under their hiding place, he saw the second guard scrambling to his feet. He was a bald pirate with huge gold earrings.

The man stumbled to the nearest cannon and fired a shot over the open sea — Barracuda Bill's salute.

Julie trembled and pressed her snout under Pip's shin.

Many feet and a couple of wooden pegs trampled onto the deck, and then Pip heard Barracuda Bill's voice. "Darn this!" he roared. "Were you trying to sink us with that cannonball? And where is my pig?"

"The pig?" The bald man looked around in confusion. He stammered, "It — it must have drowned!"

"You were supposed to stand guard, you hairless slime fish!" Barracuda Bill barked as he held out the cutoff rope. "And what is this? You think the pig was hiding a knife behind its flopsy ears?"

Pip's heart nearly stopped.

"Search the ship, you oxeyes!" Barracuda
Bill barked. "Bring me back my pig! And the
one who cut the rope!"

The pirates cursed and stumbled away in all
directions.

"Julie!" Pip whispered. "You *have* to jump,
or else those men are going to fry us!"

But Julie just hid her head between her legs.

"I'll let that pig starve for three days!" Barracuda growled. "No, a whole week! I'll lock it up with nothing but dry bread and water . . . !"

That's when Julie charged.

With a loud grunt, she ran over Barracuda Bill and shot through the bald pirate's legs. Then she flew over the railing.

Pip followed her without a second thought, past the confused pirates. He got to the railing with a couple of leaps and flung himself over, toward the black water.

Pip splashed into the sea, barely a pig's breadth away from Julie.

"I'm coming!" Stout Sam called. The dinghy shot out from behind the pirate ship, where Sam had been hiding since he'd heard the Barracuda approach.

Sam pulled the thoroughly soaked Pip and the dripping Julie into the boat, and then he leaned into the oars like he'd never done before in his long seafaring life.

"After them! What are you waiting for?" Barracuda Bill shouted from the railing. "Get me my pirate pig!"

"But—but we can't swim, Your Nastiness!" Swordfish screeched with fear. "And you can't, either!"

"Then shoot at them!" Barracuda Bill growled. He was so angry he nearly fell over the railing.

Stout Sam rowed like the devil while the pirates readied their cannons. Soon the cannonballs came flying, splashing into the water right behind their boat.

Stout Sam panted, "If their aim gets just a little better, they'll turn us into matchsticks!"

All of a sudden, Julie started squealing, so loud that she even managed to drown out the cannons.

"Dog sharks and needlefish!" Stout Sam shouted. "Julie! We don't have time to fish for treasure right now!"

But Pip dropped his oar and listened. "Captain!" he whispered. "They've stopped shooting!"

Stout Sam lifted his head and listened, too.

Pip was right. It was suddenly very still. But then they heard Swordfish's shrill voice across the water. "Your Nastiness!" he shouted excitedly. "The pig squealed. Did you hear? It really squealed!"

Pip held his breath.

Barracuda Bill's men were standing behind

their cannons with their mouths wide open. Everybody was listening.

Just then Julie threw her head back and squealed once more, so loud that Pip had to hold his ears.

"Hooooraaaay!" the pirates cheered. Pip and Sam saw them scramble to cast out their nets.

"Let's hope you're right, Julie!" Stout Sam whispered as he picked up his oar. "Would be nice if there was enough gold to keep those scoundrels busy fishing for a week."

With a grunt, Julie rolled herself up in the
bow of the boat and fell asleep. Pip crouched
down next to her and stroked her bristles.

Tired and happy, Stout Sam rowed them
back to the harbor. It was already growing light
as they tied their boat to the quay.

"Hungry now, Captain?" Pip gave Stout
Sam a huge grin.

"I'm so hungry I could eat a whole pig!"
Stout Sam answered. He quickly pressed his
hand over his mouth. "Oh! I'm sorry, Julie. It
was a figure of speech. I of course meant a whole
cake! Or two, maybe!"

Julie wasn't even paying attention. She sat
on the quay and grunted happily as the sun rose
over the sea.

"I'll be right back!" called Pip, and he ran
to the Thirsty Shellfish, where Lanky Lola was
sweeping the night's debris out into the street.

"What happened to your pig?" she asked as
Pip tried to squeeze past her.

"We got her back," Pip answered. He
grabbed the bag of jellyfish cream cakes, which
was still standing on the counter, and ran back
to Stout Sam and Julie. The two of them were

sitting on the quay, and Stout Sam was tickling Julie's ears.

"Thundering flounders! Jellyfish cream cakes!" Stout Sam said admiringly as Pip put the bag down next to him. "Where did you get those?"

"I think we earned them!" Pip answered, while Julie sniffed the bag hungrily. "Though I'm sure our troubles are only beginning. Barracuda Bill will be after Julie even more than before, now that she filled his nets with gold. I think we'll have to hide her, don't you think?"

"Yes, I'm afraid so," sighed Stout Sam. "We'll probably have to find ourselves another island."

A few hours later, they were painting Julie's bristles black and telling everybody how their pirate pig ran away. Then they set sail and went out to sea with their blackened Julie.

"What kind of island are we looking for?" Pip asked.

"One where nobody has ever heard of Barracuda Bill and his golden eye patch" was Stout Sam's answer.

They sailed for five days and six nights. Julie squealed three times during their journey, though Stout Sam never cast out his nets. They still had enough gold coins on board.

On the sixth day, they found a peaceful island where there was nothing any pirate would ever be interested in. And nobody there had even heard the name Barracuda Bill.

They picked the most beautiful stretch of beach they could find, and there Stout Sam built a sty for Julie. He planted coconut and banana trees next to it and built a hut for his and Pip's hammocks. And Pip of course painted a new sign. Then they built a jetty they could tie their boat to and for Julie to sit on and look at the sea.

And they are probably still living there.

And they are probably still very, very happy. . . .

Turn the page for a sneak peek
at another charming chapter book
by CORNELIA FUNKE

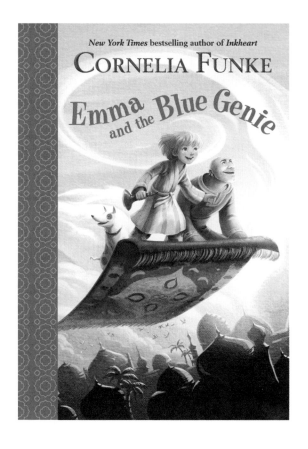

Available now!

1

THE BOTTLE IN THE MOONLIGHT

Emma loved the ocean. The house where she and her family lived stood right behind the dunes, and at night you could hear the waves rush over the sand. To Emma that was the most beautiful lullaby in the world. Her four brothers, however, thought that it sounded like a growling sea monster, and it made them dream of giant octopuses that pulled them out of their beds with wet arms.

Brothers are strange. During the day they fight and scuffle, and at night their fear of the dark won't let them sleep. Nearly every night

one of Emma's brothers crawled into her bed
to hide from sea monsters and octopuses, only
to immediately start snoring so noisily that she
couldn't hear the rush of the sea anymore.

It was on nights like those that Emma put
on her bathrobe and snuck out of the house to
trudge through the dark and down to the water.

The salty wind whispering across the waves,
the beach stretching from one end of the night
to the other, it all belonged to her alone. It was
wonderful. Four brothers can be quite hard
work for one girl, so every now and then she
really needed a little solitude.

The darkness never scared Emma. After all, she had Tristan with her. His legs might have been as short as bratwursts, and his tail might have looked like a twirly noodle, but he also had lots of pointy teeth in his mouth.

Sitting on wet sand is not very comfortable, so Emma always took a cushion with her to the beach. On that cushion Emma and Tristan sat side by side, and the sea breathed at their feet like a living thing.

On clear nights, when the moon poured a silver highway onto the water, Emma imagined that at the other end of that highway lay the most beautiful and wondrous land on earth. People rode on camels, and palm trees swayed in the warm breeze. There were no brothers in that land, or maybe a few teeny-weeny ones who were very gentle and only wanted to scuffle on Saturdays. Nobody went to school or had to work. The sun shone every day, and there was just enough rain to water the oases, which lay like shimmering diamonds at the edge of the desert.

Who knows?

Maybe the moon likes to eavesdrop on the thoughts of girls who sit alone by the sea with noodle-tailed dogs. Maybe he listens to their dreams and tries to make them come true. Maybe . . .

One night, when Emma again came trudging down the beach with Tristan and their cushion, there was a bottle floating in the moon-silvered water. It bobbed just a few steps away from the water's edge. It shimmered and flickered as though someone had stuffed it with a thousand glowworms. Emma tried to pull the bottle from the water, but her arms were at least a couple of feet too short. So Tristan waded into the cold waves.

"I wonder what's in there," Emma said, as Tristan dropped the bottle in front of her feet. "Do you think I should open it?"

The glimmering and glowing made her feel a little uneasy, but Tristan just looked at her and smacked his lips, which meant something like, "Of course you should open it!" If he'd meant, "You better not!" he would have turned his backside to her.

"Fine. If you say so," Emma said. "But it's your fault if something bad happens." Then she pulled the stopper from the bottle.

And here's a look at the next
chapter book by CORNELIA FUNKE!

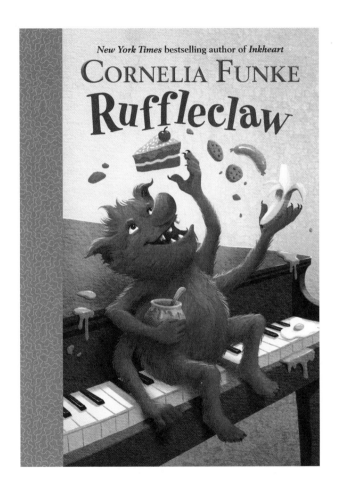

New York Times bestselling author of *Inkheart*

CORNELIA FUNKE

Ruffleclaw

Available now!

Ruffleclaw's burrow lay well hidden under an old toolshed, right next to Shaggystink's and Wormtooth's burrows. For its main entrance, Ruffleclaw had loosened three floorboards inside the shed. Outside, carefully hidden among high stinging nettles, was the emergency exit, because Ruffleclaw was an earth monster, and earth monsters were cautious creatures.

Like any other earth monster's burrow, Ruffleclaw's home smelled of earthworms and millipedes, but the floor was covered with soft sweaters, and piled high in the corners were all the human things he had snuck away with over time.

Ruffleclaw's neighbors, Shaggystink and Wormtooth, came to visit him only very rarely.

"Yuckity-icky-yuck!" Shaggystink moaned

every time he poked his head into Ruffleclaw's burrow, always holding his big nose with at least two of his four paws. "What a horrible stench!"

Wormtooth would just mutter something about human filth and quickly return to her own burrow, which was filled with the delicious scent of hundreds of woodlice.

Ruffleclaw didn't care at all what those two

thought. Let them munch their bugs and scratch their fleabites. Let them wallow in the mud and slurp slippery slugs. All of that was just not enough for him. Oh no.

While the other monsters spent their nights digging for hideous treats in the humans' trash cans, Ruffleclaw padded right up to the human house on his furry paws.

Oh, how those bright windows lured him closer. And the music! That horridly wonderful jingly-music. It made his knees go all wobbly.

Usually Ruffleclaw just peered through the windows, or he listened at the walls with his delicate ears. Sometimes, though, when the nights were particularly dark and when nothing moved in the human house, Ruffleclaw would open the big door and sneak inside. The silly lock was of course no problem for his monster claws.

And what exciting things they had in there! Ruffleclaw's night eyes needed no lights to spot all the wonders in the dark. He would grunt with joy as he rolled around on the thick carpets or dug his furry face into the soft pillows. He took the most delicious treats from the ice-cold box where the humans collected their food.

And at the end, he always went to look at the faces of the sleeping humans, staring in wonder at their naked, completely un-furry skin.

"Those humans look like mole rats!" Shaggy-stink said with a laugh. "Like huge, icky mole rats."

So? Ruffleclaw thought. Was their shaggy monster fur really any better? There were always lice and fleas in it. The humans probably never had to deal with *that.* And the humans didn't smell of damp earth, but of delicious soap. Yum!

Ruffleclaw had once taken a piece of soap back to his burrow and slowly eaten every last bit of it. It was the most delicious thing he'd ever tasted!

"You'll meet a terrible end one day!" Worm-tooth warned him. "You already smell like a human! Yuck!"

"And?" Ruffleclaw asked, his green eyes turning red with rage. "You'll see! Oh yes, you will!"

"See what?" his monster neighbors asked uneasily.

But Ruffleclaw just bared his teeth and grinned. His scrumptiously smart plan was none of their business.

ABOUT THE AUTHOR

CORNELIA FUNKE is the *New York Times* bestselling author of many magical books for children, including *The Thief Lord, Dragon Rider,* and *Inkheart.* She was once named one of the 100 most influential people by *Time* magazine. She was born in Germany and lives with her family in California.